EYES GLAZED WITH LOVE

Author Praise Mk Nkhoma
&
Co-Author Zenobia Paguntalan Abiera

PUBLISHED BY: -

GLOBAL VISIONARY PEN LEGACY
SELANGOR, MALAYSIA

<u>COPYRIGHT</u> ©

Book Title: **EYES GLAZED WITH LOVE**

Published by: **GLOBAL VISIONARY PEN LEGACY**

Cover designed by: **V DESIGN & CONSULTANT**

Copyright © 2024 Praise Mk Nkhoma

ACKNOWLEDGEMENT

I'm extremely grateful to my respectful parents
Mr. Nkhoma & Mrs. Kalua, who could never allow
me to quit.
To God, who gave me the strength to climb every
step with a compassionate heart.
My friends from close circles and across the oceans
are dearly supportive and encouraging.
To everyone who has ever loved and accepted my
uniquely creative thoughts;
Thank you to reader for making effort to buy and
reading this book.

Special thanks note;

Thanks so much, **Madam Zenobia Paguntalan**, with
deep gratitude for your collaboration. It has been
great to share these memories and experiences with
you.
Further extend to **Ms. Vimala Thanggavilo**, who
guided and supported me in this book compilation.
Your leadership and advice are highly appreciated.
For **Ms. Misty Holden**, by introducing this **Global
Visionary Pen Legacy** publisher to participate and
publish my creations.

Heartiest regards,
Author Praise Mk Nkhoma

AUTHOR PROFILE

Author Praise Mk Nkhoma is a young passionate writer from **Malawi** who has contributed a great deal in the field of literature with 200 something recognitions and has been featured in many Anthologies. He is the **Co-Founder** and **Group Expert** at the **GLOBAL PASSIONATE WRITERS.**

INTRODUCTION

"EYES GLAZED WITH LOVE", is a book written by poet Praise Mk Nkhoma and poetess Madam Zenobia Paguntalan Abiera from Philippines.

The book is a convergence of love poems where two hearts meet at a junction though miles and miles apart, cherish memories, share experiences, and mend mistakes, an adventure of two lovers unknown to each other's world.

This rendezvous manifests the potent power of irrepressible emotions as Cupid's arrow pierces vulnerable and lonely hearts.

The book will take you at the end of the tunnel of love where there's light but darkness also, joy but also sorrow, satisfaction but also longing.

<u>DEDICATION:</u>

To all budding writers who are still struggling to find their way.
My lovely readers who continuously support me by purchasing my books.

CONTENTS (1)

By: **Author Praise Mk Nkhoma** ©

EVER-PRESENT LOVE

For the one being transitory, the other is perpetual;
Let then tomorrow be the wing wherewith we shall
fly
To the treasures of heaven, a sphere special
Offering the purses of our hearts unto the sky.

Oops! The high harp of love is strung from the cell
That which never deceives or desert hope in cheer
For it's never been a vapid civility you criticize and
tell,
Not a common-place where the tunes your steps alone
can bear.

The taste of love into the very fibre of my nature
Seemed to have paused the breathe of time.
All regrets at my loss has gone down into the wind's
texture
Being touched by a delight more than self-induced
rhyme.

There is no past so long as this love shall live
It's serenity of art softens all fluxes of life
And lifts the downtrodden from their degradation
above.
Ooh pitheee be a part of my being, in a reign supreme.

Lose not the intensity of our-to-be epoch
The shoe is a match, the foot does not pinch
So carry me on the dazzling wheels of joy,
Come, as the rounding of stars ticks, so our story.

WE'RE TIMELESS, MY LOVE

Sense the heaviness of my scent from your back
The murmur of affection at my fingertips snaking
your waist
As the tiny jewels against the black velvet sing to the
world
All night until like bright specks of gold they dim into
the breeze of dawn
And the dark softens, red and orange spurts out in
suspense at sunrise.

You know, someday the new cohorts of existence
Shall crowd about how you and I used to Love
Of how often we could lose track of the nest of our
petting
And how constantly we caught the ribs of Bethlehem
in our eyes
Funny to imagine how even history would fail to read
our chapters.

Some will say we either lost pieces to our heart's
symbiosis
And so without someone's venom love would fly out
the window with time
Damn, after so many centuries what could be old
enough than time?
They'll never know how gradually the feeling has
become dearer to us than our own breathe.

We are timeless my Love, we'll tiptoe on every tick of
the clock

As for now, let's live our own verbs as they
pronounce their nouns
How the hell on earth do they think they're gonna
make it?
Let them lie blind under the blackening myths of their
experiences
Will they make it to move us? Oh! No, we'll always
live this feeling.

THIS TOO SHALL PASS

I've wrestliled with the songs I sung to live out my
life next to you
But Mama, living has become the calculus of time
with not a clue
My life has been extinguished too many times before
here writing this to you
Still a well rendered bizarre present limps to invade
my soul

A scavenger, juts my shrewish tongue out of every
sad poem
Dear life, what have you drugged me with?, this mojo
of yours dey hex me
Don't answer, it's just a question of losing things, as
inevitably they wings
A question that I've failed to rise back up and fight
with your winds

Have I even been home environned in the fair greens
of it's sphere?
Nostalgic, i see myself slipping away, down into the
muddy depths of depression
For I am an unlettered boor, without a spot in the
rudiments of life
Steeped in all my past lives is this pain severe stuffed
too deep

But is it not God who pulls a rose out of a sea of
thorns,
Gives wings to a caterpillar by the wisdom of it's
being desolate

And gives another 30 years to an eagle by going
through the pain
Of taking out it's beak and claws and feathers for a
new start?
That how I know this is to remind me that it too shall
pass, the pain.

SUPERFICIAL LOVE

I didn't die hard only to see you cocooned in this golf
of love
I wanted you to gradually but fairly grow out of love
in it's immense
With your heart's claws and fangs fittingly drilled at
my back
Erasing the usuals installed from your experience in
relationships

I didn't falter coronating you but for straightforward
and tender reasons
I believe my love is divine and not cosmic but a
cosmetic to your imperfections
Thus I hope I didn't flatter you with my pretty words
which ain't life
For to you life's tangled, twisted, writhing from it's
very burgeoning

Weave a correspondence that love is not what we do
but what we are
Would you expect me seeking to bite my teeth with
my own teeth?
Would I even see my eyes with my own eyes if not
through you?
I want you to see through the translucent mist which
hides my love's casted glittering beams

WHY WOULD YOU FAIL?

In silky beards and big pacifist eyes
Sexy brown skin shoving out leaflets
And undressing beauty in pamphlets
Waking sirens of adoration in your ears
Maybe i could have been your favorite boy
Always in your arms, a favourite toy

Breaking down crying and trembling
In the tombs of depression where light decays
At every corner of it's delight shrieking
With the sip of my own wild intoxication dying
Since then, I have always cherished the rays
Of your words, soothing rays of the sun

Dragging rocks on my knees to pave a way
Waving this brook of feelings to myself
To feel the caresses of Caribbean love
Being lost in the wet petticoats of wanting-to-have
Ooh yes , the course of love in our souls can't be
directed
It directs us, wherever it leads we follow

The oblivion of sleep being a nightmare
As I shift dreams into your picture frame
Where's the venue of all these dreams?
My mind is crowned with memories of you
The floodlights of our past emitting melodies
The truth of this longing remains to be a mystery
Why would you fail to make me your favorite boy?

IF I WERE GOLD

If I were gold in flesh, I'd be the breath of Love
Behind hurt, they would not get enough of me
Verily, i would have charmed an entire world
Froze it's ambient lobes in the unmoving mist
it's piles of quest for satisfaction interfused in wonder

They would have risen and pleaded with me
To sew up their yearnings with my button eyes
Drive them unto the arms of the Galaxy
In the dawn of every bit of life, I'd be the light
Inspiring their floral hearts into blooming

The Weaver of souls, harmonious whole
The turner of hearts from dark sweeping
conflagration
Moulder of the cosmos, much alike the paradise
Forger of time where those who venture to approach
are lost
And those dearer to the objective eyes burn to ruin
from their own dreaming

I would have given you breath so close
That you even wouldn't see it or touch it
I would have built temples to merchandise spirits
And a government of taxes for your solo benefits
Would I then bear shame for transforming these
humans
Into whatever worse or best out of their will?

CONTROLLER

Ooh friends, let me sing like a happy canary as we
dine
I really love the way she wrinkles her nose and laugh
Her presence shifts my scenes in all tastes of times
Feels so much great to be hooked this kind of the way

She dey do me like a controller but not a slave to
emotions
She permits my body to go out of control, no
composure
She carries me away as if no longer in possession of
my faculties
Should I delay to enter the church for conformation?

Like how the wind undresses the trees in winter
And adorns them with blossoms in spring
So does her accent absconds my innate whinging
Oh how her piercing eyes freezes my lips bloodless

She unearths the keys to my heart with her every
touch
She leaps into my soul, her strides more effective
Ooh God, the enrapturements of her body gestures
She makes me feel loved in precisely the way I want
to

No degree of any influence of similarity can invade
To the sky its beyond the magnitude of our
differences
I am merely in love, I've become an atom of the dust
of love

She makes me feel like aawwwh awwwh eeey

#inspired by Onesimus Muzik

FAREWELL

I guess you won't say love is a divine-granted
compensation
And sniffing it's aroma like cream on my palm's
latitudes there sketched
Ain't vanity, I pray you say love is the recurrent
cliché separating life from death
You agree? Then i hope from its grandeurs you find
peace again

If Romeo couldn't manage to spare a kiss for Juliet
I hope it's fine to let me cherish every moment of our
enchantment
That is currently chirping in suspense with the dusts
and darkly shimmering
In crimson-stained flowers which at first were happily
blossoming

How professional it was showing me only the good
and not the bad
Sharp claws and canines in your pockets, acting the
happy and hidding the sad
You were always at the crests of your lips painting
faint smiles
But you never meant them, only yellow stumps in-
between your teeth

Were you just clearing a speck from your eyes when
you winked at me?
The undulate flames of the fire you lit in my nerves
sucks a deal from my eyes

Fears, you made me think that everything I believed
was pure, true
But now every word you promised has never come
through

If you were to give me the love I couldn't give myself
If I were to feel strange in a way i had never felt....
Okay maybe you did, maybe I did, then what the hell
did just happened?
We were supposed to be here hooking fingers and
swearing
And not complaining how you made me feel like I
was difficult to love...or I did
It's fine..it is just a small world with an endless sky,
soar and find your peace

THREE WISHES

With good utterances I would have changed the world
Not while dressed in rushes of gusto or adrenalines
I would have made blunt the cusps of their tongues
Should they be cantankerous and grumpy at
themselves?
No, for the words speaks what's within the words
sometimes

Who's fully blind to not see that my ancestors lived
never to see me?
Should I not give up my breath if so to embrace the
source of the beginnings?
Since what seems to be stirs and what we claim them
to be lures
Are we to take the false for true and the true for false
or roll them around?

Ooh don't tell me that hurt is just a piece of the heart
For i may appear amidst your presence a tender
juvenal
But melancholy compounded of all my lost simples
races
Wraps me in it's humble gorges at the apex of
solitude
I admire the adventures of this pain to be at ease
This sense of crisis to give me strength and warm my
breath

Three wishes I would wish if I were to wish
To bring back the collars of humanity around every
neck

To greet my ancestors and have dinner with him who
created the cosmos
And to let out this flood of pain which I've been
holding for years

26

I MARRIED A MAN

It's ages since I saw my mirror smiling
Echoes constantly at a distant mile it's yelling
What do they care as in this league I wallow?
"Long-term marriage is patience", says my fellow

I married a man who is empty of his own likeness
Of course he flatters not to deceive me
Not like many does he fancy with my weakness
But my passion for us remains his weapon

His squeezing, my crawling, his pounding
So we do like swimmers in the sea
Rocking at the apex of the huge waves
Submissive I must be but in beating?

If wishes we're ready winged horses
I would have ridden mine into the sunset
Of my old metalled hopes which flew
Into infinity by his tongue and bring them back

Ooh! mother, I married a man of my choice
Every time I'm forced to coax the day naked
Just to bring a live plate for him to grab
I've become a seeker who will never find

YOUR LOVE IS MAGICAL

I want to smile at how you've settled our differences
I wanna write of how you've silenced my heart's
complaints
And how my love has been scolded into perfection
and harmony

When I was quite at my trust's climax, that's before
you
A violent hurricane of goodbyes surfaced ripping out
my hold
Velocity elapsed without a flush of hope
My one-to-one love relationship was slaughtered

I never thought I would be reincarnated again
To think of being birthed from the loins of love
Which I only thought waves of time washes away
into nonentity
But you, you've proved it that love at first sight
May not come at the first place

It has all started with the gestures of your care
Without straining my heart I've healed the pain
My soul warfree to float up into the sky again
Withstanding the drag as my wings measure it

A handful of times your intentions have awaken me
From some prison deep inside a broken dream
And all the cascades of twinkling beauty
Have found me easy to embrace
Your love is magical, my darling

I'LL ALWAYS LOVE YOU

On man-day, oops! I mean on moan-day
I'll cast about a peal of secret rhymes
And begrime your flesh with my deity touches
Poising your breath in ether gloriously
Such won't be called what-could-have-been

On shoes-day, ouch! I mean choose-day
I'll cloth you the gown of love to embrace the warmth
of change
Truth is my habit so I confide unabashedly to you;
Even when your sandles rolls threadbare and sere
Of trust, you'll always be what will be there to fight
for

Both on ways-day and on phase-day
I'll be a repleted story over-ahead your longings
My ways shall make my own chances for your
satisfaction
Above where birds flies by, the sky is alone and I'll
climb it's ladder for you

On try-day, ooh not again, I mean fly-day and scatter-
day
I'll glide at my own vows, a man of action and
happenings
And a the peep of every dawn I shall cover you with
my prayers
On Sunday, you'll be my prayer partner in the house
of the Lord

THE ROSE CALLED LOVE

Breaking the banks we have never made
In the breeze of confusion a decent regard
Those words of comfort spurned under
That wink of fair eyes a violent thunder

That pat on the shoulder a heavy rock
It pleases us in quietude no thought astir
Blocking the green runnels of our walk
But we always end much conferring at our own stare

We often fight hard to make love stay up
Expecting the rose to always be in full bloom
With no phases of budding or fading, no rebirth
Throat swelling somewhere between our predictions

Devoid of extraneous threads or only two
It strikes at our ease and all through
Love doesn't jump off the rack for our hold
It is tailored within our candid hearts towards our
beloved

Is it hard to stay with love in all its vicissitudes;
From bud to bloom to barrenness and then back to
bud?
Or we brood over our sentiments towards it's essence?
Love in such a huge wave demands patience

WHEN YOU'RE NOT HERE

A mind ago I completely lost myself
For one finger is not the hand
And so it takes your presence to be me
In you i see the reflection of my own gaze.

In despair's castle I am flowered with smiles
Our love is blind for it sees and faces all
Makes room for me to be me in all my grandeur
Yes, a shadow that comes before the light

I found what I lost right here in your arms
It's rose growing petals in the love you share
Then thorns in the conflicts we each day endure
And finally roots in the commitment you surface

I wanna cherish this rose with all its petals
It's beauty always folded then unfolded
It's thorns that pierce but also open me
Oooh how it hurts when you're not here

FOREVER AND A DAY

I want to love you forever and a day
To spend my time comfortably enough with you
For there's a lot of freedom to believing in your vows
Our intimacy in perpetuity churning out of a fairly
tale
The one Angles would love to read without feeling
woozy

I'm crouching behind the walls of excitement at the
locus of affection
A fictitious sense of fantasy probing along my
breastbone
For a space to drum and dance between my ribs
That is why I prefer calculus, hard to prove a theory
than it would be easier with algebra

In your enclosing arc of beauty full of womanly
quality
I wanna use a protractor to sketch angles on your
figure and prisms of us
Plunging this distance and time a fold to yield
internity
Calibrating your feelings to being permanently
fulfilled

I shall offer half my remaining time upon the earth
Just to see that velvet iridescence etched like a glow
on your forehead
For you do not only gratify the barks of my present
But ripples back in time repairing and renovating my
past

I hope it doesn't bother you when I get obsessed with
pet names
This dagger of jealous poised over my heart, I wanna
be envied for having you
Call it hardiness or selfishness that I'm asking of you
for too much
But risking your life for my own glorification is what
I'll worship you for

WITHIN WITHIN

And so i tuned every basic out
And crafted the unusuals from my heart
Finding my feet in a world much alien
Not of ready spring my pieces to redesign

I brought with me a heart unzipped
Doff my epitathy robes to the ground
Inscriptions on the gravestone of my hope
Didn't weight you to keep me in your ample bosom
and I felt whole

How can I keep back a thought of you from my
forehead?
For this veritable paradise nourishes me so well
When the world around was stolid and deaf for my
gestures to read
You lyred a many fraction of melodies I could spell

When the ebbs of life marked me sorry and plain
And senescence from toiling mimicked my breath
You showed me my live potentials from within within
And helped me cherish my scars and feel their
strength

A THOUGHT OF YOU

This uttered fragrance my garden adorns
Laps at the basement of bliss too deep
Therein cocooning anguish leaks down
And the waning candles of affection relight

Too fast rolls the wheels of our by then folded fate
So fast to realize the invasion of it's fullness
Perhaps I should have been on guard of myself
If one could ever be on guard against Love

Or it would have been worse to shatter it to ashes
And wait for the remolding of it's own composure
But can someone break the sun's wonted path
And ride to the past for his divorced reasons?

Perhaps there would have been emptiness of this
jovial vessel
Which cups my thousand morn of who I used to be
I shall persist to die more than ever before in this
Farewell all the chances of recovery be it an infection

You shower my days with much happiness
Loneliness has gone with it's withered roses
Nowadays I walk hours within me only to find your
smile
It's even hard to write a verse about myself
Without a thought of you my darling

HAD THERE BEEN A TRAILER

Internity a motionless waiting-tide
It procures a permanent anticipation
About heaven's latitudes and it's sees
And daily the flesh dirges it's own death-soughs

Discontent of unique and peerless ways within
Empty bosoms which braces sharply our fall
Not living at our personal capacity to love
As the inverted bowl whereunder we hate, goes
seaward

Humans having depths of a thousand fathom
And multicolored hearts of many intentions
Fall prey to the proselytizing murky casements
As the full winter freezes their sight entire

If my boneless fingers were to write
And leave my ductless eyes to pour a pond
I would wish if there could have been a trailer
Maybe many of the glories in this transcendental
jigsaw
Would not bloom unnoticed to our very eyes

Perhaps we would share love like a mother
Sharing her portion of life to her daughter
We are aware of this all and we know which way
leads
But we remain camouflage humans
On the leaves of hate waiting for His coming

BY MY NAME

A sign of great contentment it shall be
Baring in memory the pieces you've held together
I shall remember our faces in the dusk
And your laughters in the suspense of the night worth
pursuing

Balling my sweating fists violently together
As you rub the salt of goodbyes on my wounds
And keep under wraps my very name
The crests of this spot lifting me more than I can get

My selfish dreams, call me by that name
My attention, sensitive to my needs and feelings
Only to satisfy the full breadth of my labyrinth
Seducing your innocence for my own glorification

But the desire in your eyes all alive, I can paint them
Always falling for your-whatever hypothesis I seem
to roleplay
Shall you then break away from the life we've known?
And venture forth into the infinity seeking for
validation?

I affirm being a man who can do, of noble deeds
For I lead my path down the pastures of faith
Should doubt or pride then bend my neck from
picking the star?
Call me by your favourite name, I'll get tired too

HOW DO YOU LOVE ME?

You're all the world will try to take away from me
You're all there is that each time I got to fall in love
with you
That's always the problem in love being always love
You make sense out of my whole life and I get to
survive my agonies

Now wrapped in the tranquillity of this floral shawl
I break all my floodgates like a tsunami tryna find it's
shore
Springing out of the world's imposed solitude
How the heck a handful times I seem to had been
blind?

Cordial prurient waves wafts at a frenetic pace
For your body gestures clots my heart in melting
tenderness
I have no favourite track of record to explain this
You have a jealous voice, it drains all the songs
empty
So let my pen sketch the trails of the goosebumps you
paints

Flushes of elation masks my nerves when you're here
Your smile buoys up a racing heart in my viscerated
stomach
Unleashing this out-of-control feeling inside me
How do you love me? What basics were you taught?

THE UNSENT MESSAGES

Even though your embrace existed in rarity, you were
all I ever had
Everything which seeps infront of the present evokes
a feeling déjà vu
Every spring of our petting was champion at it's
zenith my love
Now time has drunk our endless passion, love's entity
an empty hive

Kiss not my cheeks farewell and then leave
Judge me not with your gaze and then pin with blame
my knees
I've been once a loner dreaming of romantic days
Had a few friends because my heart never grazed at
my ease

Joy fashions itself in bits of every size, that's good
news
Swelling clouds gathered plain and live, what a muse
But you were afraid of it's shades to summit blaze
We both have missed our chance with on of the lords
of love

But how much, how much does it cost to lose?
How vast is the void of patience for the manuscript of
love to close?
The book of us remains not in proses but thorny roses
Neither of us, it seems, will know it's ending phase.

I WANTED TO WRITE

I wanted to write you a poem, my Love
Charismatic verses to rattle on until hell freezes over,
It would have left the most parching thirst run
through your body,
The one you would have cherished like the last drops
of honey in a jar,
Through my lustrous and iridescent lips leaving you
gasping for more.
Ruefully, I crumpled the pages into balls everytime I
tried to,
I felt a splitting pain in the spine and my head was
brimming with baffling impulses.

It would have been a poem my love,
Full of brisking hugs and series of kisses.
I would have crooned a neutered song, kind of bland
and balmy,
Fresh and piquant to the palate of your tender feelings
As ylllou visualize your tongue melding with mine
Not my hackneyed jokes pasting canned smiles on
your face
But I was so tethered down and my eyes were glassy

Maybe tomorrow, yes, tomorrow my Love
I'll write to you a beautiful poem

IF NOT FOR THESE STORIES

The whole poem is a gibberish so leave me here
alittle.
The universe skates down from it's filters and skims
along the main
Shooing away from the spot where like pink
geranium at my balcony lies the pain
I get myself another crest full of ornery, raised in the
ghetto;
Irrevocably cantankerous and grumpy like a piece of
strife.

At times an optimist grown groggily from time's
debacles
Forging new beliefs through and through about
miracles
Still a dozen times I feel my existence being snuffed
out
The world I've always loved tugs at my faith and
pulls the curtains that shrouds my fragile heart.

Heavy eyes as if they have been glazed with Kachasu
since centuries behind
Searching for greener pastures while draining the
gusto for lassitude
Being merry in being eulogized yet my unicity
pillowed in similitude
Perhaps life would have been worse if not for this
misery...life itself.

Huffs …

"Tis still a best world with a big heart of all possible worlds
Always in rose-colored eyes at everyone, all around it some beautiful ords
Inside are lips of selfishness delighting in it's visceral core
While life lashes steam blowing in wafts across my soul.

THE BORROWED NAME

I dine on the salads of words
And call myself a star upon the sky

The fields I till are my sandals and the thatched house
my shell
Yet far in the exile of my heart's solitude I've been

Decimal in appearance but dare to reckon my rustic
soul...eeish
My rugged eyes are but a bird's body with no
plumage

Boring, I am at most times in my poems
Turning your vibe wherein your merriment lies into
something

Under the shades of my quest's branches I delight
Through verbs and phrases does my ink's happiness
nictitates

So when out of the sky poetry detonates painting the
galaxy
Hiss not the tones of your double tongues at my back

Poetry does swindle the thorns that take root in my
desert of despair
It's flute speaks melodies of life's mysteries

I WON'T BE GONE FOREVER

When my face is ashy and my eyelids drop shut
Do not say the horde of death's shadows have lifted
me to the fore
I'll be a forget-me-not blooming at your window
Seething your soul into an ocean of serenity

When the moments we shared are shrivelled
Sing an old song at the verge of it's passing out
When there remains only a little light in the day at
twilight
Do not long for a stabbing regret of wasting the
sunset alone
I'll be there filling you up, my breathe in yours

Swerve not the steering of your memory at our spot
I'll be a tormenting tornado in your life if you do
Let some credit flow as you nab my pictures close to
your breast
For our connection isn't mythical but will always be
true

Perhaps our fusion is will last with our hearts together
Who knows, don't be fed up while God can still do
The trailer's opening door is always a ferocious hero
As long as time may seem, I won't be gone forever

PEACE I LEAVE WITH YOU

When the night's dear embrace drops on my lap
And my breathe wears it's perfume like a jacket as it
blows
With it's blinding shaft without being driven by fears
Cut not your jaws agape with surprise, I'll be in the
temple hibernating

When dawn is only left ashes and echoes of birds
songs
The garden of the night shall be swept dry, never to
return
Heave a metalled sigh as if it were wrong to leave
You've been sure as I kept crawling at your
comforting lips

Not now, the coffin shall not patrol my heart set upon
waiting
The pedals of fate shall ride the perculiaty of my
absence
The beak of yesterday shall peck at your grieving
hearts
The inferno within your voice wont set me elated in
peace

So long had I been an emblem of art behind real pain
Drowning inch by inch as criticisms kept winding the
other ear
Reality was just some graffiti left unnoticed on the
face of the sun
And all I loved taught me living a hermit in the
paradise of solitariness

But peace I leave with you, my dear ones
You can paste lipless smiles on your hard faces
Just don't forget to kindle an internity of memory in
your heart
For the bird of time still remains Kiwi, never to be
able to fly
I'll be waiting beside the throne with flowers for your
arrival

WAIT FOR ME, DARLING

When a fresh lapse of the night comes lapping by the
shore
And the sun is drilled out at the mountain's peak by
the tides of the sea
Smile at the golden hues of the new sunrise bouyantly
rocking with every wave
Let grief fly with the kingfishers to nest in the west
far from home

Climb the ladders laboriously of how twinkled the
truth in my eyes those days
Wallow with your regrets at the waste in the labyrinth
of your pride
Come with your head hanging on a lance of being
sorry
My sleep shall be worth a break to wipe your tears
and kiss your cheeks

I had an ill hunch that this would someday backfire
Im sorry for I trusted the murmurs of my inner impish
instincts than to warn you
Feel not insecure that all the lilacs are now red
Your waiting shall not be in the vain pursuit for our
gap

We have had this sorted everything now and then
So, waste not an hour drinking deep the void which
has sunk through the throat of our embrace
Wait for my return with the planet's ring to marry you
For as I as do, the only necessary things left behind is
me being in you

IF I WERE YOU

I would have done this and that differently
Perhaps I might have prevented mishaps and swerved
off their course
I wouldn't have wondered why people failed me or
why I did, obviously
Maybe I wouldn't have dazed myself long enough
with ignorance

I would have done things my own way featly
Own a sun-drenched beach where echoes would
snigger briefly
Following the flowers and saffron of a summer sunset
And live in reality the dream that the sun would never
set

In the nick of time to act, I'd curb humans of their
deep heart
That they don't bargain for the graves they are fated
Make them walk steadily by faith and not by sight
And bring to life the doctrines which fades out in the
dusk

I'd have turned the passion of a flower rimmed in the
dust into a man
The blade of the grasses under my feet into his sword
The warmth of the shells and nests in a cold day into
his shield
But all these would have been my own bane
If I were to be you

INWARD LEVERS AND KNOTS

A wave from the past pummels my brain
And splashes above the rock of my fortitude
Dead ends of any kind makes me claustrophobic
Holding back this flood because I'm aquaphobic

Inside my chest bravely keeping down this pain
Whatever you call these inward levers and knots
I have been so dry for sway in my very lane
How ill at ease do you feel telling what hurts?

If I were to tell all of what I felt back and front while
there
Perhaps I'd find no bones left in the anatomy of the
air
I'd to scramble out and suck stamina in the cartilages
fixed in my limbs
Then tell you by a sniff like a dog that which life
dumps

It does not matter my current lead is a wonder
Have you ever seen how at it's very root the rainbow
is sprayed
When the sky lie in their throats to tell about thunder
And the scent of the clouds vanish to find no rain as
we've prayed?

Unpredictable yet expectable....
That's how the pain goes off....

A HEART WITHIN THE HEART

The eyelids of a calm morning
Loosens, if I get my hopes up
And pillow the day on my lap
Parading my bazooms enticingly
On its face to raise the stigmata
Of it's passion confined in a mew
Somewhere behind temptation

Hope is there but an empty vessel
An inveigling current that pomades life
An odour of existence when misery shallows
But when it's wallops misses with your face
And it laughs all the harder
It metamorphosizes into a beguiling sinister

Should there be such latitudes
That tomorrow's tenderness of the sun
And the freedom of the wind shall be fair?
How pretty much do I have to know
That what becomes a thought becomes?
Does it take a heart within the heart to act?

HEART OF MY HURT

A sad song from out the distance plays
As i discard my comprehension completely
Of things from the tranquil pond of my life
Nightly, my confidence dries with the pillows

Eternally perennial spring of purpose vanishes
It seems immeasurably obvious to the eyes
The ability to trust a man is tossed and broken
Thus i seem to rejoice in the reality of this pain

Luckily, it's something sane and of this world
It's embellishment soothes my fancies
Where this emptiness is no more empty
But it's flapping wings shadows my way

A wave much familiar hurls and rips open
With it's claws the wounds of memory
Through the forehead the dagger digs
And my whole skin throbs with pain
Should this be what i planned before?
Are expectations the source of this all?

THE BANGING DAWN

Shrinking from each of the morning's release
Brutal awakenings that quakes at my heart
The sun treads with a harsh gushing of light
I'm left feeling like I'm gasping for a breeze.

The day ahead looms heavy and dark
Each moment furnishing nothing for a spark
A great fixed chasm of dread and despair
Sluices my soul through it's merciless glare.

My shoulders hangs down from the weight of the
world, suffocating
Like I'm confined in a nightmare, forever waiting
For the dawn to break and unchain me
From this continuous skidding of misery

Survival of the fittest is the motto to live
Relief comes with sleep and flies through the window
Escaping from the grips of this hellish lodging
I finally want to mute my eyes and feel nothing

A HERO IN DISGUISE

Of course, I am to turn and ask about your care
Wondering if your toil knows "too much", my dear
Let me wash down these impulses that dies along my
throat with cheer
And paint the curtains of honor for your love which I
can't compare.

Ooh the candlelight that always shine in use
Through all dimensions of life you can't refuse
From dawn till dusk your hands etch their fate
Drinking life to the peak just to gladden my heart
I can't remember not seeing you dancing bright as a
bit over a waning day

In it's highest degrees of a day's concrete swelling
embrace
Beyond the utmost bound of the space of human
existence
From the East to the West where sinks the leading sun
You made rough your hands just to crack a smile on
that boy

Oooh the storm of felicity which always meet his
adorations
He shall not hinder the rain of his heart unto his eyes
And let grief hung tight it's knob on the door of his
throat
For he always find it hard to speak about your heart's
esteem in this stirring life

So as I wink in this hollow heart made void by some
songs I didn't get to write
I mind it well and admit it's the only way I can speak
to you
Drop me a kiss as I wheel round the past, just a boy
Look at the sketch of your own genes from it's past
Still glowing as if alive, not being touched by the
sickles of time

MY LOVE

If I were a fish
I would have swum with you
Until nightfall
And every sunrise and sunset
After that.

Not for your looks
But for the way you open my mind
And make every single stroke
Worth pursuing.

I would have walked the minutes
With you into where lowers the sun
For you fill my days with flowers
A bastion of my daily hope

Your lithe body undulates
With flexuous grace
This makes the air around
Perfectly clement

I want to hook my finger on this;
Across the gulf of time
We will still be one
For I'll always choose you

For the light you brings
For the melody in your laughter that sings
For the life your mere existence flings
I'll always choose you

ON SOME DAYS

Look on my face and forget everything
The molded trust and the threaded bonds
In this peopledom i bear no surname
Have swelled myself from trying being me

And oftentimes the pouring begins
I become familiar to most sleeping pills
Not letting go of what once was dear
How can I take back my all of me while in pieces?

Freely gunning for their terrestrial aims
As despair's tranquillity engulfs in it's fullness
What can nothingness see in the mirror?
I feel like drained of feelings to show

Call me a late-sleeping and early-waking bird
For inside this aviary the walls truly do speak
It's a monotonous invasion every dawning of a flesh
day
Maybe in vulnerability lies my key to this all?

I'M JUST A GIRL

I want to taste the danger of not sinking into this total
silence
I want to paint some sort of portraits in maybe a word
Why have i gone from feeling damp to being dripping
sad
Perhaps this sense of want shall rewrite my peace

Yes, I'm just a girl but I'm more than just a face
I have dreams and aspirations, I have my own pace
My soul is drunk and my verdure is ruined for use
Would you take advantage of a crippled heart to
bruise?

I'm tired of being held a captive in the jungles of your
estimations
I want a welcome reception and a love poem full of
affirmations
Should you continue objectifying me than who I truly
am?
I want to sing with you all sorts of songs except the
sad tunes

You only see my curves and promise you love me to
pieces
Okay I'm not familiar with music that's why I take
your words as gospel
It's fine I have feelings I can't control but I have a
beating heart too
Do you ever mind all these before thrusting yourself
on me?

You nuzzle my neck when I cry, "NO NO, please
leave me alone!"
But your voice is a gun, you inch my dress higher and
undid my bra
You stoke my engine and thump your tail leaving me
a victim
I am a girl and more than just my appearance
I am worthy of all the love and acceptance

HER APOLOGIES

With the sound of your steps dying away
So was dying the last thing in the world
That which would have always mattered
Now no appeal of emotion pities her day

No reason can unchain her from her own verdict
You lightly meant every wild word you did flog
She made your vows her fate and her heart
Became perpetually prey to your flag

Yes, she wronged you but she longed for you
You judged her err and made her bloom alone
Maybe it's you who had never understood her
She had given love wholeheartedly then lost it

Chests heaving in time with each other
Arms circled around her waist scrupulously
Where's the petting of your always-being-together?
Obviously you knew she would wither away

Had she ever understood you at her wit's end
Perhaps she would never have loved you
Perhaps she would never have lost you
Forlornly she wonders if she had ever really
understood anyone in the world

DEAR MAMA

Did you ever sleep a wink till the blooming of a soft
dawn
Or virgil apportioning lullabies to the solitude of a
toddler's sleep?
At the verge of a breezing sunset in early July
As the birds sang farewell of the glorious sun
Did your canticles perennated the launching of the
night?

Larking every morning with a dulceous and fair face
Your hair pomaded cajoling a downpour of a piercing
beauty
As life awakes and tugs it's weight at your hopes
Your eyes as if swabbed with a diamond kerchief,
unglazed despite your whole-night vigilance
The hub of a sweet home rolling steadily the wheels
of life

Verily, Dad's eyes javenlined well aware the pearl of
the planet
Did he ever tried fobbing off the trust of your adorant
feminine?
I would quickly fortune to disown his title this very
time
Need you not clot your heart with fear but confide in
my protection
For in the salons of the world your wishes I'll grant

Should hustle fly me to the moon and never return me
back

A diabolical nostalgic ache shall violently kill me
alive
I won't tread shortcut courses to gain your name
reputation
So, at this fraction of my writing-you-a-letter
Wherever you're, I just wanna salute you, my Queen

DEAR MAMA 2

Giving your life for my battles
In a wreck at a sea to save me
Your perpetual sacrifice for our tables
To quench a living death in us resting free

Ooh not for years but centuries
Have i failed in comparing your services
Your legion heart, daily fresh curries
The brook of your care which still lavishes

At times you had to remain at home
Evenings, and look after the children
When the others were out having a good time
You never ceased shining on us, the sun.

The hub of all the houseworks, not offended
There was my clothes to make or mend
Again my company to be entertained
Darning to be done, school meeting to be attended

Saw you often up working at night
Long after all of us in the house were asleep
Ooh let me owe you an ocean of credit
You deserve to be lauded and help up as a statue of
hope

AS WE GET OLD...

As the sense of life becomes heightened
And high emotional temperatures
Grips our solitary threads
Come, let's brood on it's mysteries
Than the fact of temporary existence

Let's embrace nature's beautiful prospects
Hang our griefs and feel ever much better
From the torture of trust and patience
By-and-bye there shall be us but bones
And the honey-coloured faces shall forget

Come, let's dress our hair
And throw on our favourite colours
And do otherwise what the world would do
Let's lose its familiarity like a day dream
As we feel the drag of the songs we've sung

~ Author Praise Mk Nkhoma©~

ABOUT CO-AUTHOR

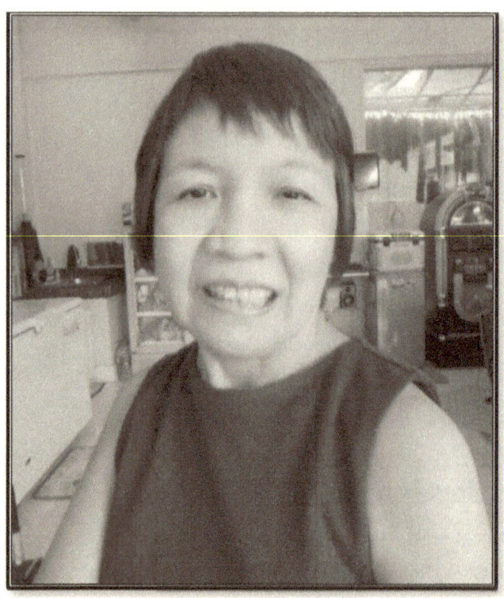

Zenobia Paguntalan Abiera is an award-winning authoress from **Philippines**. Since June 18, 2023, she has garnered a total of 413 awards in global poetry platforms and local awards in novel, short stories and chidren's rhymes.

CONTENTS (2)

By: **Co-Author Zenobia Paguntalan Abiera** ©

LOVE ESCAPED VALENTINE

Sighs fly
Drifting in the dreary February sky
Whispers of love that passed by

Birds chirp
Singing for those who weep
Love that escaped their Valentines.

Musings in the night
Voices swallowed by darkness
In the hidden valley, echoes of sadness.

Hearts down and forlorn
Curtain of love, closed and drawn
Tragedy of despondency borne.

LOVE PLEDGED ON THE SAND

When you came to visit, I thought life was grand
Love envisioned, alas on the sand
The waves caressed and whispered, I thought you
truly cared
But all your proclamations, were farce and smeared.

I built sand castles, on my heart and mind
Believing our future was entwined
But my illusions of love, was carried away by the tide
Washed out by your insincerity, defiled.

The footprints you left on the sand, pained me deeply
They were nothing but hogwash and mockery
All the songs, that you have sang for me
Were fake blabberings, of your tongue, I see.

Footprints of our love, left on the sand
Manifestations, with no fidelity at hand
I wish they would be erased, in time
Heartaches they gave me, love declined.

DIMENSIONS OF LOVE

Real love is unconditional
Tends to be multi-dimensional
All encompassing in its features
No clash of wills and fissures

Pride is never an issue
For a love that is true
Animosity written off to oblivion
Awards time for communication.

Friendships last forever
Affection perpetually linger
And in the case of lovers
Issues are cordially settled.

Genuine love by many traits described
Of symphaty, emphaty, loyalty and devotion ascribed
Be it between marital partners or friends
True love reaches out and understands.

True love never forsakes
Nor does it forget
There is never room for regrets
All these, in the heart reflect.

VAMPIRE OF BROKEN HEARTS

I am the vampire of broken hearts
I will gather sad hearts, replace them anew
If they can't be mended, hand them to me
I will gorge on them, to set you free.

I will punish all those who hurt you
I will force love potions on them in a brew
I will set up a fire and in a big cauldron
Exterminate memories, of lovers you mourn.

I will ensnare all deceitful men
Indoctrinate them in a camp
To never torment women
Teach them, love is not for fun.

And if in stubbornness, they resist change
In the dark dungeons, I will have them chained
Until the day, that realization hits them
Love is beautiful, not a toy and not a game.

FIRST LOVE

The embers of first love remain in the heart
Thought to be extinguished, through the years when apart
But the dormancy ends, when a stimulus ignites
And the heart is consumed, by an enflamed fire.

As the blaze rages, devouring the mind
The heart in turbulence, troubled and wild
Wanting to flee from the intense emotions
Enraptured by the flames, succumb to desperation.

The ghost of the past is a hard foe to battle
Debilitating one's will, its grip is hard to disentangle
The humungous force of a past love, rearing its ugly head
Is better left shunned, and forge to life ahead.

BORN OUT OF LOVE

We came to the world because of love
Ideally we all exist and thrive on affection
With no one to share, everything is bare
We need someone to cherish and to care.

Hapless is the man who stands all alone
Living a cold, lonely existence on his own
Human hearts by nature will gravitate towards love
Ti's a human need, the quest for affection.

Love is an unquenchable thirst that hearts seek
A drought of it makes souls grow weak
A life without love, loses all its meaning
Sadness eats up joy as tears keep rolling.

Love can nourish or wreck havoc and devastate
It can invigorate the psyche or may debilitate
A feeling that inspires or cause utter desperation
Love is therapeutic, at times an emotional contagion.

PULSATING HEART

The heart, with many senses
It can feel, see and hear
Loving, it visualizes, a person of perfection
Feeling rapid thumping for the object of affection.

The heart hears melodies of love and devotion
The cries and pain, the elegy of dejection
The glow of light shining in a beloveds eyes
Seen like a reflection in the colors of a prism

The heart is attuned to what the beloved feels
Sheds tears when one truly cares
It overpowers the mind in many instances
Extolling the power of love in its crevices.

SANCTUARY

You

embellish me by your presence
inspire me to carry on despite torments
breathing in colors to my world
crowning me your queen
dwelling in my thoughts and dreams

You

gift me with zest in life
I wake up in the morning with you
traversing geographical frontiers
Thought waves coursing cyberspace
Illogical, but we share realities and dreams.

I wonder what the plans are of destiny
Will our love make it through eternity
Though in oneness our hearts believe
You and I commune in harmony
In each other, we found a sanctuary.

LOVE TRANSCENDS TIME

The flame of love lingers, its embers never die
At times it flickers, but flares up in a while
Memories come and go, surging and submerging
Like the tide of life, forever changing.

Love is etched in the heart, mind and soul
The emotion taunts, continues to cajole
Something that is loved, animate or inanimate
With the passage of time, continues to replicate.

Love is not a faucet that one can open or close
Nor is it a light switch that may be turned on or off
Feelings have continuity, refusing to abscond
Love stays forever, it goes on and on.

PARADISE OR REMORSE

Never surrender to promiscuousity
Nor agree to be a mere third party
Always heed moral considerations
Avoid both shame and indignation.

Accept not offerings of fifty percent love
To share affection with a man's legal wife
To be a mistress of third wheel will generate tears
Run as fast as you could to avoid heartbreak.

True love is not shared love
Never bask in a farce affection
A real gentleman will not give false hope to a woman
Destroying her happiness with society's stigma.

Grandiose love comes with an offer of marriage
It is sweet affection where a woman won't grieve
Love with no commitment, a form of condescension
Lack of respect for a woman, treating her a recreation.

CALL ME CRAZY

Call me crazy, if I fell for you
Love is irrational, this everyone in aeons know
The brain is entrenched on a higher plane
The heart so many times, overpowers the brain.

Stupidity is rampant for many people in love
Intelligence roams, listening to dictates of the heart
An outsider sees vividly, but the lovers can't
Blindness grips the heart, mental persuasions are
shunned.

The visions blur, heartbeats grow loud and dominate
The ears grow deaf, as the mind agitates
What the brain inculcate, the heart stubbornly ignores
A person in love, submerged in emotional whirlpool.

Thus runs the story of fools in love
The rosy world is too hypnotic to ignore
The redolence of love, when sniffed in the air
Make lovers forget reason and logical thinking,
reneged.

DECEITFUL LOVE

The dewy drops, to the leaves bid goodbye
With the rising sun, spreading rays of light
Melodic tunes, permeate the lair of the heart
In along deep slumber, it awakens, at last.

In a sprightly gait, a fair dame ambled
In a dreamy, enticing land, sauntered
A patch of roses, adrift vivid in her mind
Loveliest ones, with sweetest fragrance.

In high spirits, she seemed to overlook
Alluring hued roses, have prickly thorns
Delighting in their beauty, her heart soon to bleed
At disillusionment's threshold, spurring discontent.

Dreams of love, vanishing in the air
Searing, piercing pain, ushering despair
Staggering and falling in a deep abyss
In lieu of love, a vast chasm of grief.

Teardrops of a broken heart, stained
Persisting, through eternity, claimed
A lesson learned by this sad dame
A perished love, blown by the wind.

HIDDEN TRUTH

How does it feel when someone lies
When truth is shrouded even in the eyes
Shades of truth fastidiously wrapped
That even the gaze is camouflaged.

What of a tongue that cannot be trapped
An expert in evasion tactics and acts
Swerving at every word spoken
Keeping so many things hidden.

Like a warrior wearing an armor
And a clown painted in its exterior
The heart is veiled and so is the mind
Akin to a riddle which purposely mislead.

What does it cost to tell the truth
Is it a million times more worth
Can anyone care when lies hurt
If only to serve an ulterior purpose?

POEMS ARE MIRRORS

The eyes, a smile, spoken and written words are
mirrors of the souls
Windows of insights on whether one is bad or good
External manifestations of character made evident
Through prudent observation, one with ease, detect.

Perceptions gleaned from reading a poem
Foremost indicator, of inner thoughts and feelings
Expressions flowing from the chambers of the heart
Ruminations and ramblings imbedded in the mind.

Poems lodged in countless realms of diversity
Of joy, resentment, adulation and misery
Or a perturbed mind, making admissions of guilt
Feelings of remorse, in a poem, delineate.

Many poems speak, of a love that is true
Others delve on being lonely and blue
Disquieting is when a poet confesses
Admissions of guilt on a detestable deed.

Through poetry, many culpability is purged
Wrongdoing and loathsome plots unfolded
Deplorable fruits of envy, jealousy and insecurity
Haunted by one's conscience, in the fear of hell,
berated.

Classical poet, Dante envisioned traversing the
afterlife
Giving vivid descriptions of hell, heaven and
purgatory

Yet returning to the focal point of this poetry
The context of a poem, manifests human character, in
an imagery.

Poems reflect, what a poet desires, expects and
admires
The state of the heart and of the mind, evinced
Struggles in life, in victory or in defeat
Laurels gained or unattained, poems depict.

FANTASY ROMANCE

I wonder how it is to live in the wilds
With a meek, lovable lion by my side
Perhaps a bewitched or cursed prince
Maybe, the Prince Charming of my dreams.

What would it take to tame a lion with sleek mane
Would love be enough to attain this aim
Will he love me with a love as in the fairy tales
Will I live without fear, with him near?

Could he be a Prince in a distant place
Banished by a fairy for his mischiefs
Could he be my love in a previous life
Wishing to reunite in this modern age?

Who may this enchanted lion be
May he transform to keep me company
Will he morph to human form for love's sake
Transformed, will he ask, " Please marry me"?

VOICE FROM THE PAST

Once more, I confront the past
It's light creeping o'er the dark
Singing sweetly like a lark
It is me, said he, as he embark.

I heard him whispering, it's me
Would you still let me be
I'll sing you songs you want to hear
He said as he hovered near.

Nearer and nearer, he came to me
With light resplendent o'er a tree
I shielded my eyes for his presence glared
I stood nonchalant as he continued to stare.

Voice from the past, just let me be
Leave me alone with my poetry
My life flows calmly in serenity
As I stay with rhymes that comfort me

THE FLAME BEARER

Keep burning a flame in your heart
The fire of compassion and love
To your neighbors, happiness bring
Continually, remain a blessing

A man is worth the love kept and shared
Generosity to the poor and those in need
Emphaty, sympathy, a gentle caress
To help in healing, others in distress.

For what merits a selfish man
Who is but a conceited one
He stands alone in an island
Shunning the needs of everyone.

Keep the flame of compassion alive
Let the love for your fellow men thrive
Stoke the embers never let die
Ignite affection, let them fly

FADING AWAY

Life is a drag
It creeps like a bug
I need to fantasize.

Let's lie down under a tree
Allow the breeze to blow a caress
Sleep with the scent of musky roses.

As the moon creeps up the sky
Mockingbirds sing at night
While owls hoot to vocalise.

The Eastern whip-poor- will awakens
 Nocturnal during the dark sings
Their fabled calls for mating ring.

And in an aimless sleep I drift
Watching gnomes and fairies skip
As my mind fades away to rest.

LOVE ON MID-AIR

An aftermath of virtual dalliance
Romance suspended in cyberspace
Though lovers are cognizant of each other's need
Still an amount of dread it breeds.

To love someone who is not beside you
Whose daily whereabouts no one has a clue
If messages are sent you get some cue
But otherwise waiting makes one blue.

Suspended love, illusory but felt
By a heart which with chat messages melt
An uncertain future for this kind of romance
Brings insecurities, the heart askance.

Love which relies merely on hands of destiny
Certainly knows no predictability
Emotions at the mercy of Information Technology
Feelings floating in cyberspace, a blessing or a
catastrophe.

TILL THE VERY END

Love, be there for me, when melancholy comes
Ringing in my ears, their onerous sounding drums
Share your soulful melodies, which echo gently with
the wind
Stand guard against the darkness, looming at the
crossroad's end.

In your palette, paint me an ebullient world
Charm me with endearments, all your love unfold
Immerse me in oblivion, eclipse me in your warm
embrace
Whisper honeyed words to me, with kisses interlace.

Be there for me, in turbulence and serenity
Calm the surging waves, that obstinately surround me
Be my shining star, with your cool iridescence
Cloak me with your devotion, and let me love again.

Even as my sun pales in light, and goes down
Stay, linger by my side, and hold my hand
As I transcend the realm of non-existence, when I
forever close my eyes
Do not leave, be with me, till the very end.

And I will face the Creator, smiling
Content with you, sadly watching
As I bade goodbye to you, with my tears falling
Deep in my heart I know, someday we'll meet again.

Co- Author Zenobia Paguntalan Abiera ©

ABOUT THE PUBLISHER

GLOBAL VISIONARY PEN LEGACY was founded in Malaysia to publish books globally and gather all Authors to have a one-stop platform to showcase their prose and poem. We invite experienced and new budding writers to join us in being a part of the progress and growth together. Distribution of the reading material in varieties formats of digital to printed copies such as a magazine, paperback, hardcover, e-book, audio with visual content, and video. It will available in all genres. Readers and authors will find useful content to perceive. We publish a copyright of the write-up with ISBN to protect the authors content from being plagiarized.

Social Media:

https://www.youtube.com/@globalvisionarypenlegac
y
https://instagram.com/globalvisionarypenlegacy
https://www.tiktok.com/@gvp_legacy/
https://www.linkedin.com/in/globalvisionarypenlegac
y/
https://www.facebook.com/GlobalVisionaryPenLegac
y
https://www.facebook.com/groups/gvplglobalpassion
atewriters

<u>DISCLAIMER</u>

We have done our level best to edit the write-ups and provide an error free book. We have not detected any plagiarized content. In case any plagiarism is founded, Global Visionary Pen Legacy will not be held responsible. The authors are solely responsible for work submitted.

GLOBAL VISIONARY PEN LEGACY
~Management~

Guhasakthy Thevanai Thanggavilo (Founder, CFO & ISO Internal Auditor)

Vimala Thevanai Thanggavilo (Founder, CEO & Author)

**Misty Holden
(Co-Founder,COO
& Author)**

**Johnny Abitefibiya
(Chief Digital Officer
& Author)**

<u>PUBLISHER MESSAGE</u>

We are cordially inviting all the writers to become authors by publishing their solo books for free. From the very beginning, our mission was to reward and recognize all the writers internationally. This is the least we can do as publishers to encourage and support all the writers of any age and part of the world to share their creations with readers. Many have dreams, but not all can afford to pay the cost of publishing. We are willing to fulfil their wish by publishing it internationally, without any cost involved. Royalties will be paid periodically to an author based on the sales. Let's share the platforms that benefit and reward writers as authors.

We always feel delightful about every solo book's publishing, as it's a victory for writers to make their desire come true and the publisher's mission is accomplished. GVPL will serve you the best and is always willing to learn from all our experiences to improve our services. Interested writers are welcome to join our team and expand this service globally. Suggestions and ideas are most welcome, too.

Writers who are interested in publishing a solo book may contact us via email or Whatsapp to discuss it further.

Email: globalvisionarypen@gmail.com
WA: +6012-322 0775 or +6018-646 2331
Regards,
GVPL Management

THANK YOU NOTE

Thank you to the original illustrator for sharing such an amazing image to users for design purpose. We claim the image used without violating anyone's copyright. Thank you!

Regards,
GVPL Management

www.ingramcontent.com/pod-product-compliance
Lightning Source LLC
Chambersburg PA
CBHW031440130726
47989CB00003B/1228